BY MYSELF BOOK

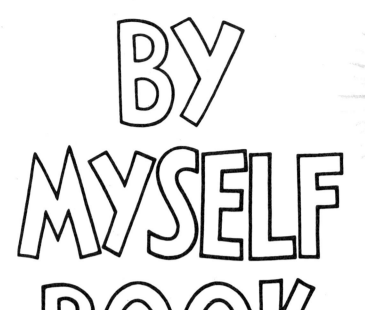

By
Deri Robins
and
Meg Sanders

Illustrated by
Charlotte Stowell

MALLARD
PRESS

CONTENTS

Mallard Press and its accompanying design and logo are trademarks of BDD Promotional Book Company, Inc.

Copyright © 1991 Grisewood & Dempsey Ltd.

First published in the United States of America in 1992 by The Mallard Press.
ISBN 0-7924-5564-9
Printed in Spain

SOLO PERFORMER

DENS, PETS AND PLANTS

INDOOR THINGS

BY YOURSELF

How well do you cope with being by yourself? What do you *do* on dull and rainy days, when your friends are all away and you can't bear the company of your brother or sister for a moment longer? Try this handy quiz to see how you shape up . . .

1. When I'm by myself, I generally:
(a) Mope
(b) Turn on the TV
(c) Grab the chance to write my first best-selling novel

2. If it's raining, I always:
(a) Complain bitterly to whoever will listen that there's nothing to do
(b) Kill time until the rain stops
(c) Rush outside in my rubber boots to try out my new design for a puddle yacht

3. When I grow up, I intend to be:
(a) President
(b) One of the first astronauts to visit Mars
(c) An inventor

4. I think brothers and sisters are:
(a) Essential
(b) Quite useful
(c) OK in small doses/a nuisance

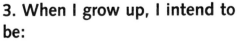

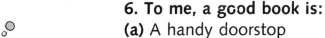

5. My idea of a really good time is:
(a) A big party with lots of games and a magician
(b) Watching *STAR WARS* on video for the fourteenth time
(c) Building a secret den at the end of the garden

6. To me, a good book is:
(a) A handy doorstop
(b) A way of passing the time
(c) A place of magic and adventure

7. My main complaint about my parents is that they won't let me have my own:
(a) Telephone
(b) Hi-fi system
(c) Private castle

8. If I was marooned on a desert island, I'd probably:
(a) Go mad with boredom
(b) Plan an immediate rescue attempt
(c) Build a cabin and learn to catch fish

... or have you heard the one about.......

Answers

?

If you scored mostly a's
Without other people you completely fall apart. One day you may *really* find yourself on a desert island with only a parrot for company – so find out how to have fun by yourself, now, before it's too late!

If you scored mostly b's
You cope quite well with being alone – but you don't really make the most of it. Try taking a break from the TV and try out some of the activities in this book – you'll soon see what you've been missing!

If you scored mostly c's
You are obviously a natural "by myselfer" and will go on to achieve great things. This book is just what you've always wanted – enjoy it!

☆This is Me!☆

ME (Finish the picture and make it look like you...)

Name: _____

Address: _____
_____

Country: _____

Continent: _____

Planet: _____

Tel. No: _____

Birthday: _____

Star sign: _____

Nickname: _____

Pets: _____

Hair (draw it in)

Arm length: _____

Eye color: _____

How many teeth: _____

What's on your favorite T-shirt? (draw it in)

Height: _____

Shoe size: _____

Length of leg: _____

I am (tick relevant boxes):

- [x] Small
- [ ] Tall
- [x] Gorgeous
- [ ] Hideous

- [x] Brilliant
- [ ] Dumb
- [x] Cheerful
- [ ] Miserable

- [x] Generous
- [ ] Mean
- [x] Friendly
- [ ] Shy

- [x] Lively
- [ ] Lazy
- [x] Weird
- [ ] All of the above

Best friends:

1. Mer Cocks
2. Michelle
3. Katherine

Things I want to achieve before I am 12:

1.
2.
3.

When I grow up I want to be:

teacher

The best film I ever saw was:

_?_

The worst one was:

_?_

The thing I am best at is:

Math

My least favorite lesson is:

Science

I am saving up for:

The best pop group in the world is:

Their best record was:

My favorite color is:

The animal I would most like for a pet is:

Cat

The best book I ever read was:

My secret ambition is:

The person I admire most is:

I admire him/her because:

If I could have just one wish, it would be:

To have 1,000 more.

My favorite sandwich is:

My pet hate is:

My favorite TV program is:

My most embarrassing moment was:

The worst thing I ever did was:

A PLACE OF YOUR OWN

BEWARE! HAUNTED CASTLE

Up until now, you may have foolishly thought that your bedroom was just somewhere to sleep. In fact, your room can be a smuggler's den . . . a pirate's cabin . . . a jungle clearing . . . above all, it can be somewhere PRIVATE of your very own. Even if you share a room, you can have fun with your own corner. The following pages show you how.

In spring, plant an unshelled peanut in a pot near a window.
Keep it warm and see how tall it grows —
You'll be amazed!

Make an A-Z scrapbook
(page 32)

Choose your own view (page 11).

Make a chest for your treasures (page 12).

Make sure no one reads your secret diary (page 13).

This is a secret diary.. KEEP OUT!

PIRATE'S CABIN

This room idea is for you if you secretly yearn to sail the seven seas in search of adventure. Follow the ideas in the picture below. Other great room themes include: witch's cave (or Dracula's den); circus; space station; the scene from your favorite adventure film, TV show, or ballet.

Make a treasure map look old by tearing the edges and coloring it brown with cold tea or paint.

TREASURE MAP

Cut out a ship's wheel from cardboard. Push a thumbtack through the center and pin to a piece of cardboard hooked over the back of a chair.

To make a pirate's hat — Cut out 2 identical hat shapes from black card and stick them together, (leaving the bottom edge open). Cut out a skull + cross-bones from white paper and glue it to the front of the hat.

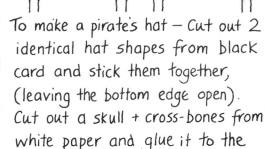

Make an eye patch from black cloth or paper. Thread a loop of elastic through each side, and adjust to fit your head.

Telescope- make two different sized rolls from cardboard, stick them together and paint.

Ship's cat

Folded cardboard

Secret supply of ship's biscuits

Pirate's trunk — see Treasure Box (p.12)

Circles of cardboard covered with shiny foil make good pieces-of-eight.

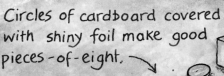

A room with a view...

Bored with the view from your window? Make up a new one instead! Here are some ideas to start you off . . .

◀ Draw around a trashcan lid onto a piece of cardboard and cut out. Paint a porthole scene like the one shown here. Or, just cut out the outer ring, and stick a piece of greaseproof paper onto the back. Use felt-tipped pens to draw your scene, and hang up in a window.

▶ To boldly go where no space traveler has gone before, make an intergalactic starship window. Paint a black sky on cardboard, and when this is dry glue on lots of stars and planets cut out from shiny kitchen foil.

▶ Make a control panel from a shoebox covered in kitchen foil, with thumbtack knobs.

◀ Go back in time to the age of the dinosaurs! There's a Stegosaurus peering through this window — choose your favorite dinosaur from an illustrated book (try your library), and copy it carefully. Tips on copying pictures are given on page 27.

KEEPING SECRETS

Here are some valuable tips for keeping intruders away when you're working on a top-secret assignment . . .

TREASURE BOX

You'll need: a shoebox; thin cardboard; foil; black paint; tape; glue, and clear varnish.

1. Tape the lid to the box. Cut shapes from the cardboard, and glue all over the box to make a pattern.

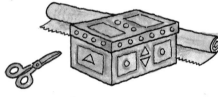

2. Cover the box with glue. Lay a piece of foil over each surface, and press down firmly. Trim the edges when dry.

3. Now cover the foil with a layer of black paint. After a few minutes, polish off most of the paint. Finish off with a coat of varnish.

A SIGN FOR YOUR DOOR

You will need: about 6 pieces of cardboard, each the same size: a needle and thread; a clip.

1. Stack the pieces of cardboard together, and use the needle and thread to make two loops, as shown. Tie the loops in a knot at the top.

2. Write different messages on both sides of each card.

3. Hold the cards open with a clip, and tie outside your door.

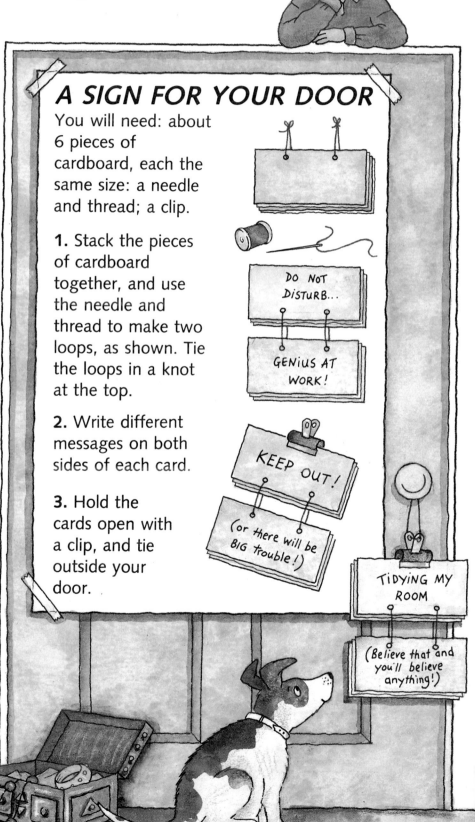

DO NOT DISTURB...

GENIUS AT WORK!

KEEP OUT!

(or there will be BIG trouble!)

TIDYING MY ROOM

(Believe that and you'll believe anything!)

SECRET DIARY

As well as your top-secret diary, you will need: some thin cardboard, folded in half, scissors and glue.

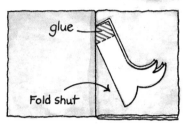

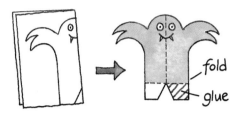

1. Copy the ghost shape above, at a size that will fit into your diary. Cut it out, and put glue onto the right-hand flap.

2. Open your diary to the first page, and stick in the ghost so that the glued flap lies along the middle crease.

3. Put a little glue on the back of the other flap. Close the diary, and leave under a heavy book until the glue has dried.

S.E.C.R.E.T. C.O.D.E.S.

1. Write out your message on a scrap of paper (1). Write it again, keeping the letters in the same order but splitting them up differently (2). Now write each of the "words" backward (3). Finally, add a misleading letter at the beginning of each "word" (4). To decode, just reverse the process.

1. COOL KIDS USE CODES
2. CO OLKI DSU SEC ODES
3. OC IKLO USD CES SEDO
4. TOC BIKLO SUSD OCES ASEDO

2. Write out the alphabet. Now pick a letter (our example uses "C") and write this under "A." Carry on writing the rest of the alphabet. To write in code, simply use the bottom letter instead of the top one. Q.M.?

A	B	C	D	E	F	G	H	I	J	K	L	M
C	D	E	F	G	H	I	J	K	L	M	N	O
N	O	P	Q	R	S	T	U	V	W	X	Y	Z
P	Q	R	S	T	U	V	W	X	Y	Z	A	B

13

·ONE· Wo·MAN· BAND·

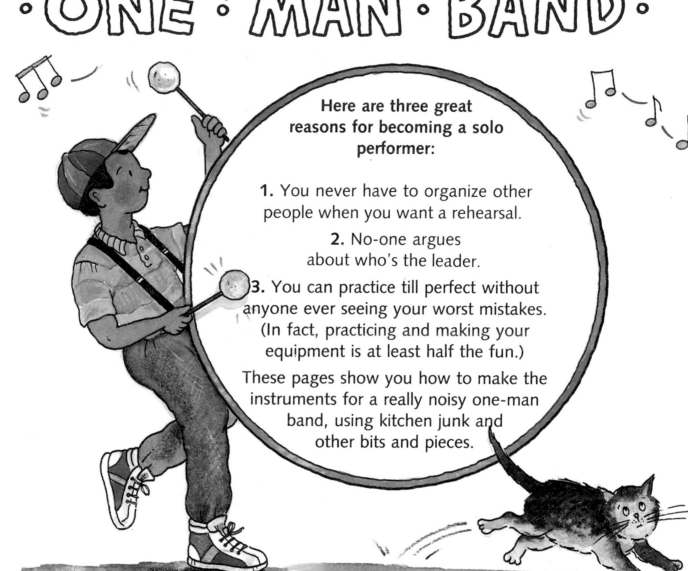

Here are three great reasons for becoming a solo performer:

1. You never have to organize other people when you want a rehearsal.

2. No-one argues about who's the leader.

3. You can practice till perfect without anyone ever seeing your worst mistakes. (In fact, practicing and making your equipment is at least half the fun.)

These pages show you how to make the instruments for a really noisy one-man band, using kitchen junk and other bits and pieces.

TOOTER

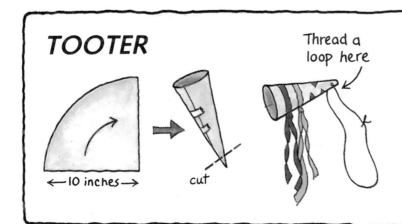

Thread a loop here

← 10 inches →

cut

Cut a shape like the one shown here out of thin cardboard. Roll up into a cone, and make a tiny hole at the thin end. Tape firmly in place. Use a needle and thread to fix a loop of thread to the thin end, so that you can hang the tooter around your neck.

BELLS AND CYMBALS

Use string to tie metal saucepan lids and cutlery to a wide belt. You can swipe at these with a wooden spoon, or just wiggle your hips to make a very satisfying noise.

Tie little bells to string for a jangly anklet.

DRUM

Tape down the lid of a large cookie can, and put it into a plastic or net shopping bag. Keep it firmly in place by tying and taping as shown. Tie string to the handles, making a loop that fits comfortably around your neck.

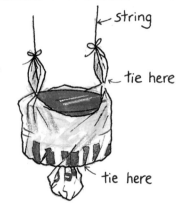

tape

You could put dried peas or beans IN the tin to be extra noisy!

string

tie here

tie here

KAZOO

You'll need a comb and a thin piece of paper. Hold the paper behind the comb, making sure that it is gently stretched flat. Open your lips, and press the comb softly against them. Now "sing" a tune against the comb (don't just blow – you need the vibrations from your voice box to make this work).

paper

blow here

ZOO ZOO
ZEE ZOO
ZOO-OO-O

TOOT!
TOO-OOT!

Use a spoon as a drumstick

Jam jar lids taped to string

Clang!

Jingle

Tinkle

JUGGLING

To make juggling balls, you'll need 3 (clean) socks, dried beans, a needle and thread.

1. Cut the end off the socks.

2. Fill the socks about ¾ full with the beans.

3. Sew up the ends.

4. Pull the thread through, and knot tightly.

JUGGLING WITH TWO BALLS

1. Start with ball ① in your right hand, and ball ② in your left hand.

2. Throw ball ① in an arc toward your left hand

3. Throw ball ② toward your right hand before ball ① arrives in your left hand.

4. Catch ball ① as soon as ball ② is in the air. Ball ② now becomes ball ①. Start again.

JUGGLING WITH THREE BALLS

1. Start with balls ① and ③ in your left hand, and ball ② in your right.

2. Throw ball ① toward your right hand

3. Throw ball ② toward your left hand before ball ① arrives in your right hand.

4. As soon as you have caught ball ① throw ball ③ toward your right hand over the arc made by ball ②

5. Catch ball ② in your left hand.

6. Catch ball ③ in your right hand. Start again from the left hand side.

17

TRICKS to ASTOUND and AMAZE!

The golden rule for performing tricks is to PRACTICE until you can practically do them in your sleep. Otherwise, you may find that the joke's on you . . .

MIND GAMES

The clue to this trick is so mind-numbingly simple that you have to do it FAST and talk quite a lot while you do it to distract your audience.

Tear a piece of paper into nine equal pieces. Do this in front of your audience, and lay them out as shown.

Ask someone to make a mark on the middle square, and to turn over the pieces and shuffle them while your back is turned. When you turn around, you will instantly spot the marked square and turn it over, to gasps of amazement from your audience.

How did you know? The center piece was the only one with FOUR torn edges!

COOL COIN FLIP

Start by balancing one coin on your bent elbow. Straighten your arm quickly, catching the coin in the hand of the same arm as you do so. When you've mastered this, try it with two coins. When you can catch three, you're ready to astound the world and you may leave the privacy of your bedroom.

WOW!

SLEIGHT OF HAND

Take a wand or pencil in your left hand, and grasp your left wrist with your right hand. Now straighten your right forefinger so that it holds the wand against your left palm, and slowly spread open the fingers of your left hand. Amazingly, the wand appears to stick to your hand by magic!

MAGIC ACES

Hand someone a pack of cards, and ask them to shuffle them thoroughly. Now take the cards, and hold them behind your back. Without looking, bring out each of the aces, one at a time!

You are able to manage this truly amazing feat because you have of course removed the aces before handing over the pack. The aces are held in place with a paper clip, and attached to the inside back of your sweater with a safety pin. All you do is reach for them one by one while holding the rest of the pack behind your back.

WH-A-A-A-T??

You will need: an uncooked egg, a packet of Jell-O, a funnel, and a pin.

Carefully stick the pin into the thin end of an egg. Do the same at the wide end, then carefully make this hole bigger – about the size of a dime. Hold the egg over a bowl, and blow down the thin end until the yolk and white slide out of the wider end. Rinse out carefully and leave to dry.

Make up the Jell-O, following the instructions on the packet. Leave to cool for five minutes, then pour into the egg through the big hole, using a funnel. Prop up carefully in an egg cup and leave in the refrigerator until set. Turn upside down to serve.

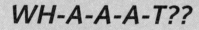

the Great Outdoors....

How would you like to go on safari in Kenya, or sail up the Amazon in a canoe? Quite a lot, we know. In the meantime, can you be absolutely sure that you've explored all the possibilities of your own backyard?

Your yard is probably home to more types of wildlife than you think. You can also have a lot of fun planting your own flowers, like the ones on page 23. But to begin with, here's how to build the best outdoor den ever.

Fold up the lid flaps and tape corners for extra height.

First of all, you're going to need the biggest cardboard box you can find. Something like a washing machine or refrigerator box is ideal, so ask in your local electricity showroom. If you can't find a big enough box, collect some large boxes from your supermarket and tape these together.

Make sure your box is big enough to make a house....

.. Not big enough!

ROOF

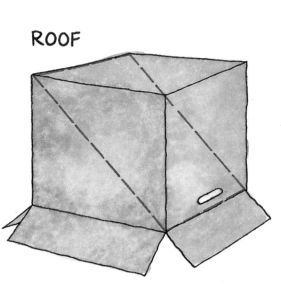

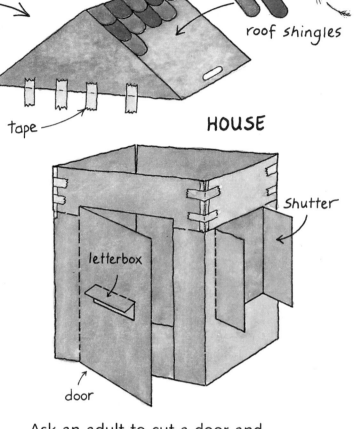

roof shingles

tape

HOUSE

Shutter

letterbox

door

You'll need another large box for the roof. Ask an adult to help you cut it in half as shown (to cut thick cardboard it's easiest if you first "score" along the line you want to cut with a knife, using a ruler as a guide). Tape the roof to the house, as shown above right.

Cut shingles from cardboard, paint them, and glue in an overlapping pattern along the sides of the roof.

Ask an adult to cut a door and windows in the sides of the house. Some of the windows can have shutters (see above and next page). Others could have a hatch, like the one on the left. And why not have a letterbox in the door?

Paint the house in bright colors — emulsion paint is best, but poster paints are OK too. See if you can borrow a proper house painting brush, like the boy in this picture.

hatch

Use your imagination to make more home improvements. You could also use boxes to make tables and chairs, or even a cooker and washing machine . . . Clotheshorses, wooden chairs etc. are also useful if you want to build an extension.

For shuttered windows ask an adult to cut lines as shown, and bend out the flaps.

T.V. antenna (coathanger)

For a chimney, push a cardboard roll through a hole in the roof.

(Extension for a friend)

Towel or rug for porch roof

Doorknobs – push a pencil through the door, and glue a thread spool onto either side.

A garden hideaway is ideal for observing all the goings-on in your garden – it's also a great base for picnics!

Growing things outdoors...

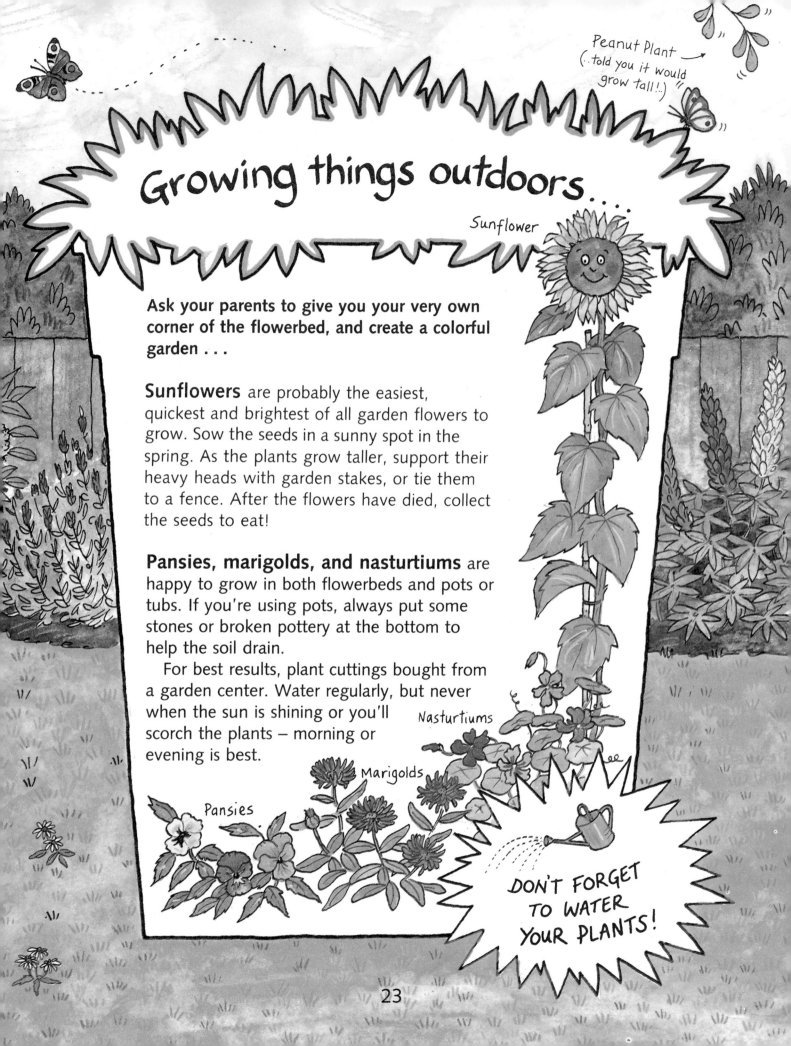

Peanut Plant → (..told you it would grow tall!.)

Sunflower

Ask your parents to give you your very own corner of the flowerbed, and create a colorful garden . . .

Sunflowers are probably the easiest, quickest and brightest of all garden flowers to grow. Sow the seeds in a sunny spot in the spring. As the plants grow taller, support their heavy heads with garden stakes, or tie them to a fence. After the flowers have died, collect the seeds to eat!

Pansies, marigolds, and nasturtiums are happy to grow in both flowerbeds and pots or tubs. If you're using pots, always put some stones or broken pottery at the bottom to help the soil drain.

For best results, plant cuttings bought from a garden center. Water regularly, but never when the sun is shining or you'll scorch the plants – morning or evening is best.

Nasturtiums

Marigolds

Pansies

DON'T FORGET TO WATER YOUR PLANTS!

Part-time pets

lovable puppy

Thinking of getting a pet? Dogs and cats make great companions, but need a lot of care and affection. Just as interesting and a lot less trouble are the animals that live wild in your yard. You can invite them to visit by leaving out tempting bits of food, and have a lot of fun finding out how they live.

BIRDS

Encourage birds to visit your yard by hanging string bags filled with unsalted nuts and birdseed from the branches of a tree. Other favorite snacks include pieces of coconut, bread, and bacon rind. A wide shallow bowl filled with water will be used gratefully for bathing as well as drinking! Find somewhere well away from cats to put it.

Size:
color:
song:
date:

BIRD SPOTTER'S NOTEBOOK

Keep a note of the birds that visit your yard. Practice sketching them, and write down the main features of each one – how big is it? What kind of beak/walk/ song/markings does it have? Find out the names and habits of the birds from a bird spotter's guidebook.

HEDGEHOGS

In some countries, people put out milk or cat food for hedgehogs. They tend to come out at evening time, when they unroll their prickly spines and trot around in search of food. Hedgehogs look cute, but they are not invited into houses — those spines are home to hundreds of fleas!

FROGS AND TADPOLES

Scoop out frogspawn from ponds in spring, and take it home with plenty of the water and pond weed you found it in. Keep it in a wide fish tank, and have a few large stones sticking out of the water. Give your tadpoles a daily sprinkling of fish food when their legs begin to grow. Return them to the pond when they've turned into tiny frogs.

frogspawn | 3 days after hatching | 4 weeks..... | 10 weeks..... | 12 weeks..... | 16 weeks

BUTTERFLIES

Butterflies only visit certain flowers and bushes. You'll always see butterflies around a buddleia tree, for example, as well as clover, brambles, and thistles. They like honeysuckle and nettles, too. If you don't have any of these in your yard, plant some wild flower seeds (which attract bees as well as butterflies). Keep a note of what you see.

buddleia

honeysuckle

bramble

nettle

thistle

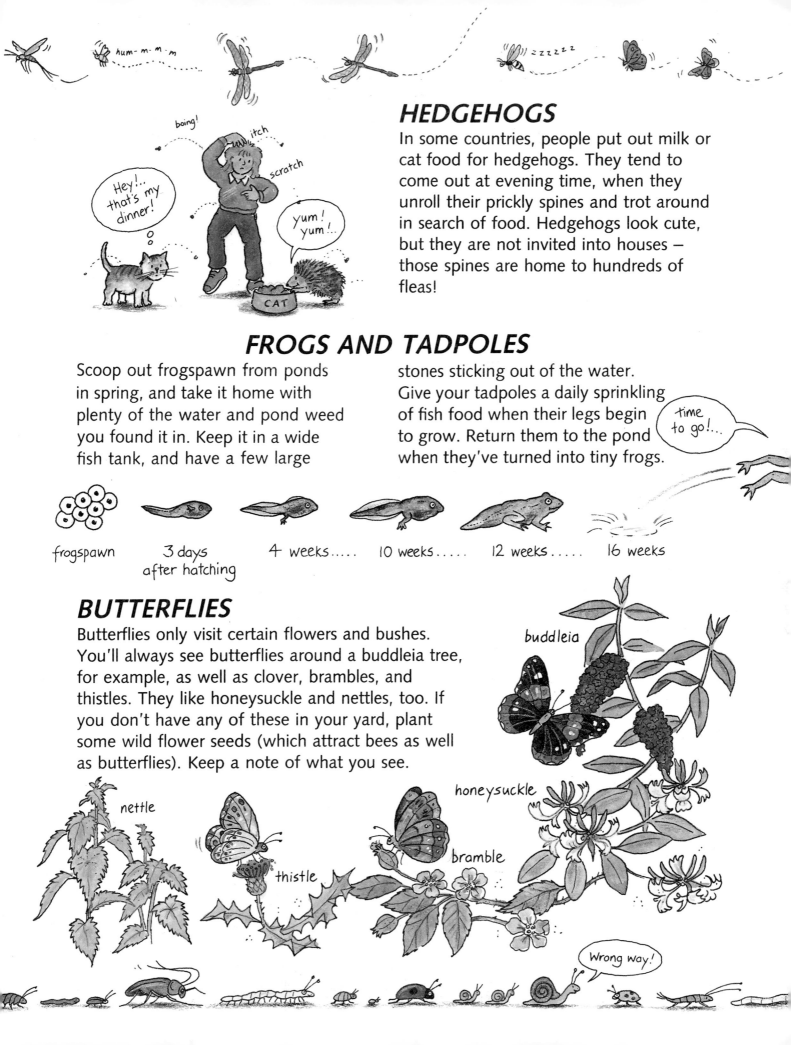

QUIET STUFF

Did you know that you were secretly a brilliant artist? Surprised? Even if you haven't sold any paintings recently, you'll be amazed at the results you can get by following the ideas on these pages. They're all great fun, especially on a quiet afternoon when there's nothing much else to do.

SELF-PORTRAIT

First, lay the side of your face onto a piece of plain paper, and carefully draw around your profile.

Using a pencil, lightly mark in the main features of your face – hairline, ears, eyes, mouth, etc. Instead of painting the features, glue all kinds of materials onto the picture – use dried beans and pasta from the kitchen as well as scraps of cotton and wool. You can make all kinds of pictures in this way. Try a clown's funny face, or maybe a scene.

DRAWING WITH A GRID

To copy a favorite picture, first divide it up into squares of equal size, using a ruler and a pencil. Now draw another grid, using the same number and size of squares, onto a separate sheet of paper. (If you want to make the copy twice as big, make the squares twice as big too.)

Mark in the main points of the picture where they cross the lines of the grid. Then copy each square in detail.

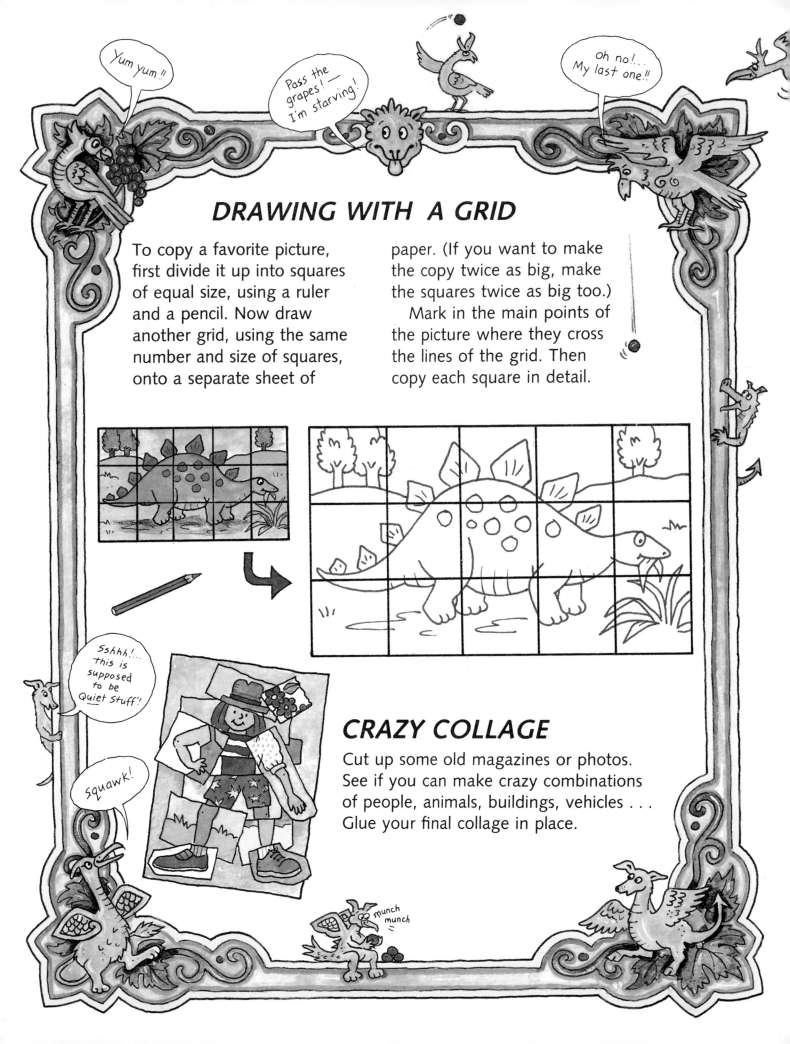

CRAZY COLLAGE

Cut up some old magazines or photos. See if you can make crazy combinations of people, animals, buildings, vehicles . . . Glue your final collage in place.

CARD GAMES FOR ONE

Take a break from noisy family card games, and try out these quieter games of solitaire. All you need is a deck of cards and some time to kill. For the purpose of the two games shown here, the king counts as 13, the queen as 12, and the jack as 11. All the other cards count as normal.

Try building a house of cards

Hee-ee

THIRTEENS

Using a well-shuffled deck, deal out 10 cards in two rows as shown above. To play, keep removing any card or combination of two cards that add up to 13 – for example, you could take away the king, the queen plus the ace, the eight plus the five, and so on. Put these cards to one side, and replace them with new ones from the pack, until you have used up all the cards. If you get stuck, try dealing out 10 more cards on top of the ones you have left.

What's all this nonsense about 13 being unlucky?....

aghh!!

SNAP!

CLOCK PATIENCE

Deal out 12 cards face downward in a circle, as if they were marking the numbers on a clock face. Deal another card face downward in the center of the circle. Now deal out the rest of the cards in the same way, so that there are four cards in each pile.

First, turn up the top card in the center. If this is a 3, for example, slip it face upward at the bottom of the pile at three o'clock. Turn up the top card of that pile, and place it under the right pile for that number.

Carry on until all the cards are facing upward, in the places shown below.

The cards should come out like this.

who's stolen the tarts?!

Ha Ha!

(Dog of hearts)

Pick a card!

Pass the spade please..

A Message to the Future

Do you ever get fed up with being told by older relatives how wonderful their childhoods were? Were the summers really always so hot, and the winters always so snowy? One way of making sure that *your* memory doesn't play you tricks when you reach their great age is to make a time capsule for the future . . .

You'll need a scrapbook, and lots of recent photographs. You'll also need the odds and ends listed on these pages.

▶ Turn to the first page of your scrapbook. Select a recent picture of yourself, and make the page look something like this . . .

▶ Now divide the next four pages up into days of the week. Starting from next Monday, keep a detailed diary from a typical week in your life. Don't forget to write in the date and the year.

This Is My Life:
Name: _____
Age: _____
date: _____
← ME

Monday

Wednesday

Tuesday

Thursday

NAME: Spot

AGE: 2

GOOD POINTS:
Friendly, loveable, playful.

BAD POINTS:
Chews shoes, chases the postman, sometimes bounces too much.

...pinches my food...

◀ Collect or take some photos of your family. Stick them in the next pages of your scrapbook, and write their names and a short description of them underneath. Include their best and worst points. Don't forget the family pets!

SPACE BUS

► Where do you live? Stick in a picture of your house. Try to get hold of a local street map, and draw your own version of it with special places of interest to you. Keep any bus or train tickets you buy this week, and stick these in.

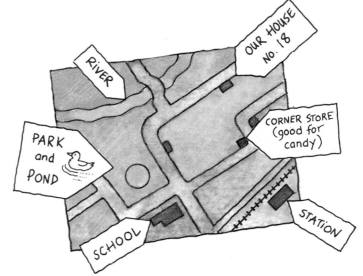

◄ What's your school called? List all your teachers, along with their nicknames, and the names of all the kids in your class. If you've got a photo of any club or team you're in, stick it in.

► Keep a list of everything you ate this week. List all the books you've read recently, as well as the films and TV programs you've watched. What did you think of them? Stick in a page from a comic and the headlines from a paper.

◄ Finish off with an autograph page – ask everyone you know to write or draw something funny. Finally, put the book in a big can or box, with any other souvenirs you won't miss for twenty years or so. Seal it up – and address it to the future!

Things to do when there's nothing to do....

1. Make a jigsaw. Cut a big picture from a magazine, stick it onto cardboard, and cut into jigsaw shapes.
2. Practice writing with your other hand.
3. Learn to whistle.
4. Use face paints to give yourself a monster face.
5. Learn something off by heart (a funny poem or some amazing facts – bet they come in useful one day).

6. Start a collection of something.
7. Start a secret diary.
8. Practice your juggling.
9. Make an A–Z scrapbook of your favorite subject. Find a photo and some facts for every letter in the alphabet, and paste into a scrapbook.

10. Make a giant pinboard. Cut a shape out of thin cardboard, and stick some cork, thick cardboard, or polystyrene to the back. Paint the front, or cover in felt.
11. Write a review of the best movie you've seen this year, and design a poster for it.

12. Make a newspaper front page, with sensational stories about your family and friends!
13. See how many words of two or more letters you can make out of your full name.
14. Make a shield. Knights used to carry shields showing pictures of things their family were good at. Your shield should show your own particular likes and hobbies.
15. Make a list of things to do when there's nothing to do!